Sometimes you're happy.

Sometimes you're sad.

Sometimes you're good.

Sometimes you're bad.

Sometimes you're scared.

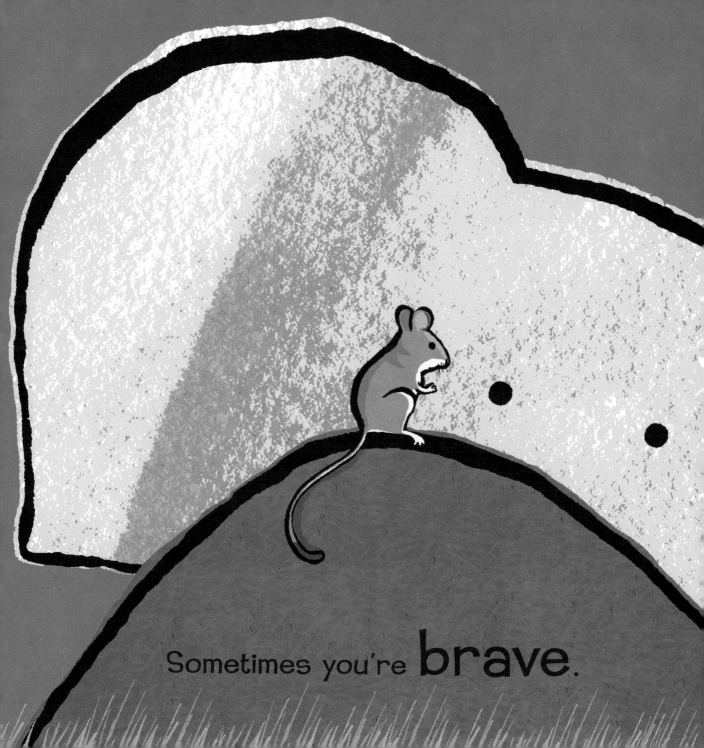

Sometimes you're brave.

Sometimes you don't know
how to **behave!**

Sometimes you're **dirty**.

Sometimes you're **clean**.

Sometimes you're
kind.

Sometimes you're **mean**.

But no matter **what** you say or do,

it makes no difference . . .